Indian Heritage
Celebrating Diversity in My Classroom

By Tamra B. Orr

Fountaindale Public Library
Bolingbrook, IL
(630) 759-2102

21st Century
Junior Library

Published in the United States of America by
Cherry Lake Publishing
Ann Arbor, Michigan
www.cherrylakepublishing.com

Reading Adviser: Marla Conn MS, Ed., Literacy specialist, Read-Ability, Inc.

Photo Credits: © Evertime / Shutterstock Images, cover; © CHAINFOTO24 / Shutterstock Images, 4; © NIKS ADS / Shutterstock Images, 6; © Mila Supinskaya Glashchenko / Shutterstock Images, 8; © Intellistudies / Shutterstock Images, 10; © Olga Vasilyeva / Shutterstock Images, 12; © Curioso / Shutterstock Images, 14; © Quanthem / Shutterstock Images, 16; © Nicoleta Ionescu / Shutterstock Images, 18; © Vladimir Melnik / Shutterstock Images, 20

Library of Congress Cataloging-in-Publication Data
Name: Orr, Tamra, author.
Title: Indian heritage / by Tamra B. Orr.
Description: Ann Arbor : Cherry Lake Publishing, 2018. | Series: Celebrating diversity in the classroom | Includes bibliographical
    references and index. | Audience: Grade K to 3.
Identifiers: LCCN 2017035944 | ISBN 9781534107359 (hardcover) | ISBN 9781534109339 (pdf) | ISBN 9781534108349 (pbk.) |
    ISBN 9781534120327 (hosted ebook)
Subjects: LCSH: India—Juvenile literature.
Classification: LCC DS407 .O77 2018 | DDC 954—dc23
LC record available at https://lccn.loc.gov/2017035944

Cherry Lake Publishing would like to acknowledge the work of The Partnership for 21st Century Skills.
Please visit *www.p21.org* for more information.

Printed in the United States of America
Corporate Graphics

CONTENTS

Almost 4.5 million people live in the city of Kolkata.

Incredible India

India is part of Asia and is about one-third the size of the United States. It has 1.3 billion people. That's a lot of people! This means India has several very crowded cities, often called **megacities**.

Many people from India have also **emigrated** to other countries all over the world. There are more than 2 million **immigrants** from India in the United States! What is their home like? Read ahead to find out!

"Namaste" can also mean "I see the divine in you."

Namaste

Walk down a busy street in one of India's megacities. Cars are honking, and bicycle bells are ringing. People are talking, laughing, and shouting.

As you walk, people may pass by and say, *"Namaste."* They usually bow slightly as they say it. Their palms will be pressed together in front of their chests. "Namaste" is a Hindi word. It is a way to say hello and goodbye.

The characters in the Hindi alphabet look much different than the letters in the English alphabet.

Most people from India speak English. They also speak a language called Hindi. But India is known for having as many as 1,000 languages! Each village has its own way of speaking. So do small and large cities. The language you speak depends on what part of the country you're from!

Applying colored powder to the forehead is part of some Hindu rituals.

One God, Many Forms

Almost everyone from India shares the same religion. It is Hinduism. Hinduism has been around for thousands of years. More than 1 billion people on the planet are followers. Most of those people live in India.

Hindus believe in one god named Brahman. But they also believe this god takes on many different forms. They believe Brahman is found in everything in nature. Hindus also

Cows are rarely used for food in India.

believe that there is a part of Brahman in every person. In Hinduism, the cow is **sacred**. It is not unusual to see cows wandering around cities. They can go wherever they want, including into traffic. Hindus believe they should not harm other creatures. This is why a number of people from India are **vegetarians**.

Turmeric can be bright yellow or orange. It has many health benefits.

Rice, Spice, and Mangoes

Do you like spicy food? Have you ever eaten something made with **turmeric**, ginger, or **coriander**? If so, chances are those spices came from India. Almost three-quarters of the world's spices are produced in this country.

Almost every Indian dish involves some kind of rice. Rice is either in the main dish or on the side. India is one of the world's biggest rice producers.

A mango lassi is a popular drink made from mangoes, yogurt, and spices.

Have you ever tried a mango? In India, the mango is known as "the king of fruits." Every spring, dozens of varieties of this fruit ripen. For a few brief months, mangoes of all shapes, sizes, and flavors are available. They are sold in Indian markets and shipped to other countries. Mangoes are stirred into rice and baked into pastries. They are also cut in pieces and eaten raw.

Create!

Did you read about a spice you have never tried? Ask your parents if they have that spice. If so, smell it. Does it smell good? Then, look up a simple recipe that uses that spice. Maybe you can make turmeric tea or coriander rice.

India produces more than three times as many
movies as the United States.

Lights...Camera... Action!

India is the number one producer of films in the world. It produces between 1,500 and 2,000 a year. These movies are made in almost every part of the country. The language used depends on which city produced the film. The movie industry in India is called Bollywood.

India celebrates many holidays. Diwali, or the Festival of Lights, is celebrated for

The Kumbh Mela Festival brings Hindus together to bathe
in the waters of a holy river.

five days. Indians welcome in good fortune for another year. As the festival begins, the cities light up. Families light candles and oil lamps and keep them lit all night. Fireworks explode overhead.

Look!

Look at this photo of people at the Kumbh Mela Festival. It is the world's largest gathering of people in one place. In 2011, the crowd was so big, it could be seen from space. What would it be like to be in a crowd of millions? Which parts would be fun? Which parts might not be?

GLOSSARY

coriander (KOR-ee-an-dur) a plant related to parsley with leaves and seeds used as herbs

emigrated (EM-ih-grayt-id) left your home country to live in another country

immigrants (IM-ih-gruhnts) people who have moved from one country to another and settled there

megacities (MEG-uh-sit-eez) cities that each have at least 10 million people living there

sacred (SAY-krid) connected to God or gods

turmeric (TUR-mur-ik) a plant related to ginger, used to add flavor and color to dishes

vegetarians (vej-ih-TAIR-ee-uhnz) people who do not eat any meat

Indian Words

Hindi (HIN-dee) a main language in India

namaste (NAH-mah-stay) a greeting in India

FIND OUT MORE

BOOKS

Apte, Sunita. *India.* New York: Children's Press, 2009.

Chakraborty, Ajanta, and Vivek Kumar. *Let's Celebrate 5 Days of Diwali!* Chicago: Bollywood Groove, 2016.

Perkins, Chloe. *Living in ... India.* New York: Simon Spotlight, 2016.

WEBSITES

Cool Kid Facts—India
www.coolkidfacts.com/india/
Read more about life in the seventh-largest country in the world.

National Geographic Kids—India
http://kids.nationalgeographic.com/explore/countries/india/#india-tajmahal.jpg
Find information about India's people, geography, language, and more.

Science Kids—Country Facts
www.sciencekids.co.nz/sciencefacts/countries/india.html
Learn more interesting facts about India.

INDEX

ABOUT THE AUTHOR

Tamra Orr is the author of hundreds of books for readers of all ages. She graduated from Ball State University, but moved with her husband and four children to Oregon in 2001. She is a full-time author, and when she isn't researching and writing, she writes letters to friends all over the world. Orr enjoys life in the big city of Portland and feels very lucky to be surrounded by so much diversity.